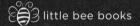 little bee books

251 Park Avenue South, New York, NY 10010
Copyright © 2018 by Little Bee Books
All rights reserved, including the right of reproduction in whole or in part in any form.

Library of Congress Cataloging-in-Publication Data
Names: Newton, A. I., author. | Sarkar, Anjan, illustrator.
Title: Trick or cheat? / by A. I. Newton; illustrated by Anjan Sarkar.
Description: First edition. | New York, NY: Little Bee Books, [2018]
Series: The alien next door; book 4 | Summary: Zeke spends Halloween in
his true alien form, but when a jealous classmate decides to stop him from
winning the school costume contest, Harris and Roxy must save the day.
Identifiers: LCCN 2018035287 (print) | LCCN 2018041139 (ebook)
Subjects: | CYAC: Extraterrestrial beings—Fiction. | Halloween—Fiction. |
Costume—Fiction. | Friendship—Fiction. | Ability—Fiction. | Science fiction. |
Classification: LCC PZ7.1.N498 (ebook) | LCC PZ7.1.N498 Tri 2018 (print)
DDC [Fic]—dc23 | LC record available at https://lccn.loc.gov/2018035287

Printed in China RRD 1120
ISBN 978-1-4998-0584-0 (hardcover)
First Edition 10 9 8 7 6 5 4 3 2 1
ISBN 978-1-4998-0583-3 (paperback)
First Edition 10 9 8 7 6 5
ISBN 978-1-4998-0585-7 (ebook)

littlebeebooks.com

For more information about special discounts on bulk purchases, please contact Little Bee Books at sales@littlebeebooks.com.

THE ALIEN NEXT DOOR

TRICK OR CHEAT?

by A. I. Newton
illustrated by Anjan Sarkar

little bee books

TABLE OF CONTENTS

HALLOWEEN'S COMING

HARRIS WALKER RUSHED NEXT door to his friend Zeke's house on Sunday. Harris and Zeke had only been home for a week following their adventure at Beaver Scouts camp, but already it felt like a million years ago. Halloween was coming this week, and that was all Harris could think about.

"Guess what?" Harris asked excitedly when he joined Zeke in his room. "It's almost Halloween!"

"Hall-o-what?" Zeke asked, repeating the unfamiliar word.

Harris smiled. He had become such good friends with Zeke that sometimes he forgot that his next door neighbor was not from Earth.

"They don't have Halloween on Tragas?!" Harris asked.

"Correct," said Zeke. "What is it?"

"Everyone dresses up in costumes," Harris explained. "For that one day, you can be whatever you want to be—a ghost, a monster, an animal, an object. Anything you can imagine! Then we all go trick-or-treating."

"What does that mean?" Zeke asked.

"We go from house to house and get candy," Harris said. "And the whole neighborhood is decorated with ghosts and cobwebs and other spooky stuff. Then we come home, watch scary movies, and eat our candy. It's the *best* holiday!"

Zeke looked puzzled. "So, once again, like when we were telling scary stories around the campfire on our scouting trip, we *want* to get scared because it's . . . fun?"

"Exactly!" Harris said. "Now you get it."

"I'm still not sure I do," Zeke said. "But I want to learn all I can about Earth culture. And I do appreciate you helping me make my way through your strange customs."

"Oh, and I almost forgot the best part," Harris continued. "Every year at school, we have a costume contest! All the kids and teachers dress up in Halloween costumes, and then the kids compete to see who has best costume."

"I'm not sure why people would want to dress up in costumes," Zeke said. "But I do like competitions. Back on Tragas, we had contests to see who could levitate the heaviest load, or who could navigate a pebble through a bunch of moving rings."

"That sounds really cool! Do you know what you want your costume to be?" Harris asked.

Zeke smiled. "Well, If I understand you correctly about this costume contest, I don't think I need a costume at all," he said.

Harris was confused. "What do you mean?" he asked.

"I'll just go as myself!" Zeke announced.

HARRIS WAS VERY CONFUSED. *How can Zeke go as himself for Halloween? He may be an alien, but he just looks like a normal kid.*

"I'm not sure you understood what I said about dressing up for Halloween," he said. "The whole point is to *not* look like yourself, to dress up as something different, or something funny, or scary."

Zeke smiled. "I do indeed understand. There's something I haven't told you about myself yet," he said.

I know that he's an alien. I know he comes from the planet Tragas and that he has some pretty cool powers. But what hasn't he told me? Harris wondered.

"The way I look," Zeke began. "I mean the way I look now, like a human, that's not the way I really look."

"What do you mean?" Harris asked, more confused than ever.

"My human appearance is only a disguise," Zeke explained. "People from Tragas have the ability to change our appearance. We can make ourselves look like the inhabitants of whatever planet we're currently on. This is very useful when my parents and I move from planet to planet for their research. It allows us to blend in."

Harris had to sit down. Somehow, this was even more shocking to him than learning that his new friend really was an alien.

"So, if this is not what you really look like," he asked, "what *do* you really look like?"

"I'll show you," said Zeke.

Zeke took a deep breath and raised his arms above his head. His body started to vibrate, then glow with a faintly yellow gleam. His skin and features softened into wavy lines, and then he began to grow taller and taller.

Harris looked up in amazement as Zeke completely changed shape.

The yellow glow faded, revealing Zeke's purple skin. His human arms disappeared, replaced by six tentacles extending out from his shoulders. His human facial features completely vanished. His ears were two antennae pointing up from the sides of his face. His hair disappeared, revealing a bald green head.

He had no legs, and was floating above the ground. His five eyes all were looking at Harris.

Harris was stunned. He couldn't believe that this was what his friend really looked like!

"It's still me, Harris," Zeke said. His voice was unchanged. "I'm still the same Zeke."

"Um, not exactly," Harris said. Then both boys cracked up laughing.

"You know what I mean," said Zeke.

Harris smiled in wonder. "Hot dog!" he suddenly exclaimed.

Zeke looked confused. "What does any of this have to do with the beef shaped like a log that we cooked up at the campfire at scout camp?" he asked.

"Hah, it's just an Earth expression," Harris explained.

Zeke nodded, then quickly transformed back into his human form.

"Well, *you* obviously don't need to make a costume," said Harris. "Just go as your true self, and you'll win easily! I've never come close to winning!"

"What was your costume last year?" Zeke asked.

"I was a superhero, but this year, I want to be a robot," Harris said.

Zeke thought for a moment, then smiled.

"I have an idea," he said. "And if it works, you'll have the best costume!"

THE TWO FRIENDS HEADED downstairs to the workshop in the basement of Zeke's house. Large metal tubes, electric wires, and weird-looking circuits were spread all over the floor and workbench.

"What's all this?" Harris asked.

"My dad and I like to tinker with some of the Tragas technology we brought from home," Zeke explained. "I'm pretty good at building stuff."

Zeke levitated some long metal tubes, some flashing bulbs, and a whole bunch of wires above their heads. Harris watched in amazement, and his friend got to work assembling them in the air.

As he finished each section, Zeke lowered the completed metal pieces onto Harris. More and more, Harris began to look like a robot.

The robot's body was a square box cut to fit tightly against Harris's own body, complete with blinking dials and knobs. The arms and legs were metal stovepipes attached to his body. For the head, Zeke used what looked like an old TV. He attached a small metal rod to look like a bright antenna.

"Pretty good," said Zeke, stepping back and looking at his creation.

"I want to see!" Harris rushed back up to Zeke's room and looked into a mirror.

"Wow!" he said. "This is amazing. I really look like a robot!"

When Harris turned around, he saw that Zeke had again transformed into his true alien body.

"But I still think you're going to win the contest, Zeke," he said.

Downstairs, the front doorbell rang. Zeke's mother called up to them: "Zeke, Harris, your friend Roxy is here!" she shouted.

Harris froze. "Oh, no!" Harris said. "This is bad, this is really, really bad!"

"I don't understand," Zeke said. "Usually you are happy to see Roxy."

Harris heard footsteps bounding up the stairs.

"There's no time to explain, but Roxy is going to be so mad," Harris said.

A few seconds later, the door swung open. Roxy started talking before she was even in the room.

"Harris, I called your house and your mother said you were at Zeke's, so I rushed right over. I have such a cool idea for our Halloween costumes this year," she said, stepping into the room. "Wait 'til you hear this. I—"

Roxy stopped short at the sight of Harris in his robot costume and Zeke in his alien "costume."

"I can't believe you made your costumes *without me*!" she cried.

ROXY GLARED AT HARRIS, shaking her head. "Harris! We *always* do our costumes together!"

"I'm really sorry, Roxy," Harris said. He removed his robot head. "I was just teaching Zeke about Halloween, since they don't have it on Tragas. Then I told him about the costume contest, and he helped me with my costume, so I—uh—helped him with his, and this just kind of happened."

I wish I could tell her about Zeke, but I can't. I promised.

"You know, it's not very nice of you to leave me out," Roxy continued. "I'm happy that you and Zeke have become friends."

"Me too," said Zeke, turning two of his five eyeballs toward Roxy.

"But where does that leave *me*?" she asked.

"What do you mean?" Harris asked, starting to feel a bit ridiculous having a serious conversation while still in his robot costume. "We're still friends, Roxy. Just because I'm friends with Zeke doesn't mean we're not still friends."

"You two go to camp together, you make your costumes together, when you know we always do that together."

"Yeah, but—"

But Roxy wasn't finished.

"And don't forget, Harris," she continued, "that *I* was the one who was friendly to Zeke first. *I* had to convince you to be friends with him. You were too busy trying to prove that he was an alien."

Harris and Zeke remained silent.

She's not really wrong about any of this, Harris thought. *Even if I was right about Zeke!*

"I'm sorry, Roxy," Harris said. "I really am. I didn't think."

Roxy walked toward the door. She stopped, turned back, and looked at Zeke.

"Nice alien costume, Zeke," she said. "You better watch out or Harris might turn you in for being a real alien."

Then she turned and left.

Once Roxy had gone, Zeke changed back into his human form.

"Did I do something wrong?" he asked Harris.

"I don't think so," Harris replied. "Every year since we were little, Roxy and I have made our costumes together. I guess I was so stunned by seeing what you really look like and excited about how you could make my costume, Roxy never crossed my mind. I never meant to leave her out. I just lost track of everything."

"Maybe Roxy can dress up in a costume that goes with ours," Zeke suggested. "Then we can all go treat-tricking together."

"It's trick-or-treating, but yes, I think that's a good idea."

Harris felt better, but he worried that Roxy might not want to go trick-or-treating with him. And he was sad that for the first time since before he could remember, he and Roxy didn't work on their costumes together.

5 COSTUME DAY

ON WEDNESDAY, THE HALLOWEEN costume contest finally arrived. All the kids excitedly streamed into school in their costumes. The halls and classrooms were filled with witches, goblins, vampires, zombies, werewolves, mummies, cowboys, pirates, princesses, ghosts, ninjas, and animals of all types.

Harris clanked his way into school wearing his robot costume. Zeke came in behind him, displaying his true alien form in public for the first time since he arrived on Earth.

As soon as Zeke entered the school, he could see kids pointing at him.

"It's a little scary but actually kind of fun to be out in public in my true form," Zeke whispered to Harris.

"Don't worry," Harris said. "Just keep pretending that it's a costume. Nobody will suspect it's real."

"Wow! That's the best alien costume I've ever seen," said a girl dressed like a zombie. "How are you floating like that?"

"Uh, there's hover technology built into the bottom of the costume, obviously!" said Harris.

"You are *so* going to win the contest," said a boy dressed like lion.

"Thank you. I think Harris has a cool costume, too," Zeke said, pointing two of his tentacles at Harris.

"Whoa, nice robot," said the lion, looking over Harris's costume. "That's really cool! Maybe you'll actually win the contest instead of him!"

But not everyone was as impressed by Zeke's "costume."

A third-grader named Jeremy Jenkins walked up to Zeke and Harris in the hall. He wore a detailed monster costume, complete with fangs, claws, bulging eyes, and shiny, purple fur.

"These are the best costumes you guys could get?" Jeremy sneered. "They look cheap and homemade! My parents bought me this awesome monster costume. It was the most expensive one in the store."

Jeremy turned to Harris. "You look like a broken microwave," he said.

Then he pointed at Zeke. "Are you supposed to be an alien? You look like a giant green peanut. And those eyeballs are *soooo* fake!"

"*I've* got the best costume," Jeremy snarled. "And *I'm* going to win the contest!"

Harris saw Roxy looking at them from down the hall. She appeared concerned. But when she met eyes with Harris, she quickly turned around and walked away.

HARRIS TOOK HIS SEAT IN MATH class. He found it hard to get comfortable with all the metal pipes on his arms and legs. He removed his helmet and tried to focus on the lesson.

Ms. Milton, the math teacher, walked into the room. She was wearing a kangaroo costume, complete with a long tail and a stuffed toy baby kangaroo bouncing up and down in her pouch. She looked out at her classroom full of wizards, monsters, and ghosts.

Zeke picked up a pencil with his tentacle and tried to write.

"What's the matter?" asked Dave Barrett. He sat next to Zeke and was dressed in a skeleton costume. "Don't aliens use pencils?"

Zeke said, knowing Dave wouldn't believe him, "Actually no, we don't. We usually use our minds to write things down."

Dave chuckled and all the bones on his costume shook.

Ms. Milton smiled. "Settle down, class. You all look wonderful!" she said. "But we still have to complete today's lesson."

Ms. Milton wrote a math problem on the board.

"Does anyone have the solution?" she asked.

69-27=

A girl dressed like a dolphin raised her flipper.

"Yes, Maria," Ms. Milton said.

"The answer is 42," Maria said, her dolphin mouth flapping open and shut as she spoke.

"Correct," said Ms. Milton. She turned to write the answer on the board, but her long kangaroo tail knocked a stack of books off her desk and onto the floor.

"I can see that it's just as hard being a kangaroo as it is being an alien!" she said, bending down to pick up the books as all the kids laughed.

At lunch, the cafeteria looked like the world's biggest costume party. Dinosaurs ate lunch next to witches, and a giant daffodil was seated next to a walking fish.

Harris took his usual seat next to Zeke. Zeke did his best to pick up a fork with a tentacle, but it slipped out before he could get some food on it.

"On Tragas, we use a long, thin utensil to eat with," Zeke whispered. "It easily rests on our tentacles. Or we can just levitate it up to our mouth, if we want."

Roxy walked over to their table. She was dressed in a sorceress costume, complete with a tall hat, a flowing orange and black gown, and a glowing magic orb. Her usual chair next to Harris and Zeke was empty, but Roxy kept on walking right past them to the opposite end of the table and took a seat there.

She must still be mad at me, Harris thought.

Zeke and Harris looked at each other. Harris decided to be brave and speak to her.

"Cool costume, Roxy," he said.

She turned away for a moment as if she didn't want to talk to Harris, but then turned back.

"Thanks," she said quietly.

Well, she spoke to me, Harris thought. *That's something.*

A few minutes later, Jeremy walked past their table carrying his lunch tray. He stumbled and his juice spilled all over Zeke.

"Oops," he said. "So clumsy of me. It can be hard to navigate in this amazing costume."

Jeremy stared at Zeke, expecting to see Zeke's costume ruined by the juice. But instead, the juice was absorbed right into Zeke's real skin.

"What—what happened to the juice?!" Jeremy asked, surprised.

Harris looked at Zeke. How was he going to explain this?

"My costume is made of special waterproof material," Zeke said.

"Oh well, lucky you," said Jeremy, moving along to his table.

Roxy slid her lunch tray down and took her usual seat next to Harris.

"Did you see that?" she asked. "He spilled that juice all over Zeke's costume on purpose! He was trying to ruin it."

"It could have been an accident," Zeke said.

"Yeah, he probably just tripped," Harris added. Roxy seemed more mad at Jeremy than at him, which made Harris feel better.

"Well, I don't buy it," Roxy said, looking upset and almost scary in her sorceress costume. "I think he was trying to ruin Zeke's costume for the contest!"

7

RECESS

AT RECESS THAT AFTERNOON, a bunch of witches, goblins, and superheroes started a game of tetherball. Most of the kids had to take off parts of their costumes to be able to play. A pile of claws, capes, clown faces, and magic wands sat in a large pile on the side of the tetherball court.

Jeremy, with his monster head and claws off, called out to Zeke.

"Hey, Zeke!" he shouted. "Wanna play?"

"Sure," Zeke said. He floated over to the court.

"You probably have to take off your costume, right?" Jeremy asked.

Nearby, Roxy leaned over and whispered to Harris. "Jeremy wants Zeke to take off his costume. I bet he wants one of his friends to hide it or rip it or something when Zeke isn't looking!"

"I don't know," said Harris. "Everyone took off parts of their costumes."

"That's okay. I can play with my costume on," Zeke said.

"I think you'd do better with your costume off," Jeremy insisted. "Why don't you take it off? I just want it to be a fair game. Don't want to beat you too badly!"

"You see?" Roxy whispered on the sidelines.

"Hmm, Jeremy *is* being kind of pushy about it," Harris agreed.

"I'm fine like this," Zeke said. "Let's play."

Jeremy scowled, then started the game.

Using his tentacles to whack the ball again and again, Zeke easily won the game.

"I was just taking it easy on you," Jeremy said, then he snatched up the rest of his costume and stomped off.

On the way to his final class of the day before the contest, Harris stopped in the bathroom. He walked into a stall, closed the door, and heard some other kids come in. Although he couldn't see him, Harris clearly overheard Jeremy's voice.

"I can't let that new kid, Zeke, win the contest," Jeremy said. "My costume is still clearly much better, but I don't want to take any chances!"

"So what are you going to do?" asked the kid Jeremy was talking to.

"I snuck a sack of flour out of the cafeteria," Jeremy said. "I'm going to use it to ruin Zeke's costume!"

"Good plan!" said the other kid, snickering.

Roxy was right about Jeremy! Harris thought. *I've got to warn Zeke!*

8 SABOTAGE!

ONCE HE HEARD JEREMY LEAVE,
Harris rushed out of the bathroom
to find Zeke. He ran down the hall,
turned a corner, and ran right into
Roxy.

"Careful! Where are you rushing
to?" asked Roxy.

"You were right about Jeremy!" Harris said urgently. "I just overheard him talking in the bathroom. He plans to ruin Zeke's costume by dumping flour all over it!"

"That's terrible!" Roxy shouted. "We have to find Zeke and warn him."

Harris and Roxy hurried through the school looking for Zeke. After searching the halls and classrooms, they finally spotted him at the far end of a hallway. He was about to go into the gym for his final class of the day. But before they could reach him, they saw Mr. Mulvaney, the gym teacher, come up behind Zeke.

"Let's go, son. You don't want to be late for class do you?" Mr. Mulvaney said to Zeke.

Zeke pulled open the gym door. He sensed something falling from above his head. Before he even knew what it was, Zeke used his powers to redirect it so it wouldn't hit him. He hoped that whatever it was would land harmlessly on the floor.

But instead, it fell right on top Mr. Mulvaney. A cloud of white exploded right on the gym teacher's head, and Zeke looked over to see him covered in flour. Some flour had also landed on Zeke.

Zeke spun around, sending his tentacles wrapping around his body. "Mr. Mulvaney! Are you all right?" he asked.

"Who would pull such a prank?!"
Mr. Mulvaney asked, brushing flour
angrily off his shoulder.

"I don't know," said Zeke. "It looks
like I got some on me, too."

"Don't worry, I'll get to the bottom
of this!" said Mr. Mulvaney. Then he
stormed off to clean himself up before
class.

Harris and Roxy, who had seen all of this, rushed up to Zeke. They quickly filled him in on Jeremy's plot to ruin his costume.

"Then that was meant for me!" Zeke said, realizing what had just happened.

"It sure looks that way," said Roxy. "Jeremy is trying to cheat to keep you from winning the contest."

"That makes me mad," said Zeke. "I really want to beat him now!"

"Looks like you got some flour on your costume," said Harris pointing to a few patches of white on Zeke's tentacles.

"I'll clean up after class," said Zeke, then he headed back into the gym.

"Did that bag seem to fall strangely to you?" Roxy asked Harris. "Like it almost changed direction in midair?"

"Uh . . . no!" Harris said nervously. "Let's, um, get to class!"

When classes ended, all the kids streamed toward the auditorium for the costume contest. Harris and Roxy arrived backstage along with the other contestants.

Harris smiled at the collection of costumed kids.

"Where's Zeke?" he asked Roxy, looking around for their friend.

"Maybe he's still in the bathroom cleaning off the flour," Roxy said.

"He's taking a really long time," said Harris, now getting a little worried. "I'm going to check on him."

Zeke stood in the bathroom, wiping the last of the flour off his tentacles and stomach.

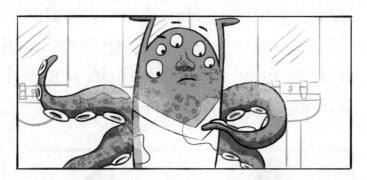

Once he was clean, he headed to the door. Wrapping a tentacle around the doorknob, he turned and pushed. The door didn't budge.

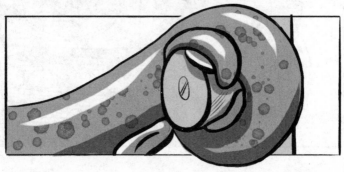

Hmm . . . that's strange, he thought. He pushed again, harder, but still the door wouldn't open. *Oh, no! I'm stuck in here! I'm going to miss the contest . . . and Jeremy is going to win!*

9 THE CONTEST

HARRIS RUSHED TO THE BATHROOM. When he got there, he was stunned to see a chair propped up against the the door, wedged under the doorknob.

Harris pulled the chair away and flung the door open. He found Zeke inside, hovering back and forth nervously.

"Harris!" Zeke cried. "I couldn't open the door."

"That's because someone propped a chair up against it out here," Harris explained. "And I think we both know who did it."

"I can't understand why Jeremy would go to so much trouble to cheat just to win the contest," Zeke said. "I want to win, too, but cheating? What do you even get for winning?"

"The top three get a small medal, and the overall winner also gets a get-out-of-homework-free pass to use once."

"That's it?" Zeke asked. They both laughed.

"Well, there's bragging rights, too. We've got to stop him!" said Harris.

The two friends ran back to the auditorium, with Harris's robot legs clanking and Zeke's tentacles flapping.

Backstage, they caught up with Roxy and told her what Jeremy had done.

"We have to stop him before the contest starts!" said Roxy.

Harris, Zeke, and Roxy found Jeremy.

"You've been trying to ruin my costume all day! You tried to spill juice on it earlier," Zeke blurted out.

"And then you tried to drop flour on it. And you locked Zeke in the bathroom when your first plan failed," Harris added.

Jeremy pulled off the head of his monster costume and smiled.

"Who . . . me? You have no proof!" he said.

"Attention, contestants!" came an announcement over the backstage loudspeaker. "The contest is about to begin. Please come to the stage."

"Excuse me," said Jeremy, slipping his monster head back on. "I've got a contest to win!" Then he walked toward the stage.

"What are we going to do now?" asked Harris.

"I've got an idea to stop him," said Roxy. "Follow me."

Roxy, Harris, and Zeke ran onto the stage and over to the judges' table. The judges were teachers in the school, including Mr. Mulvaney.

"Jeremy Jenkins is a cheater!" Roxy said, pointing just offstage where Jeremy waited.

"What makes you say that, Roxy?" asked Ms. Milton, still in her kangaroo costume.

"He tried to ruin Zeke's costume by spilling juice on it," Roxy said.

"And he also tried to get Zeke to take his costume off during recess so he could steal and hide it," added Harris.

"And then he propped a sack of flour over a door so it would fall on me and ruin my costume," said Zeke.

"Well, it fell on me, instead," said Mr. Mulvaney, still obviously annoyed. "But how do you know that Jeremy did all those things?"

"I overheard him talking about his plan," Harris added.

"That's a lie!" said Jeremy, who came running out onto the stage.

"Really?" asked Mr. Mulvaney, getting up to take a closer look at Jeremy. "Then why do you have flour all over your shoulders? Zeke and I were the only people who got hit with it. But someone who lifted a sack over his head would most likely also have flour on him. . . ."

Jeremy looked down at his shoulders. He cringed at the sight of flour stuck to his purple fur.

"You, young man, are disqualified for cheating!" said Mr. Mulvaney. "You and your flour can go wait in the principal's office!"

Jeremy, still in his monster costume, hung his head and shuffled out of the auditorium.

The contest finally began. One by one, kids in their costumes paraded onto the stage and past the judges.

Roxy marched across the stage, her long gown flowing, her magic orb glowing. As each kid had their turn, the audience of students, teachers, and parents applauded. The judges scribbled notes about their costumes.

A gasp filled the auditorium as a huge dragon lumbered out onto the stage. It was eight feet long. Its tail waved back and forth. Streams of red ribbons flickered from the dragon's mouth, giving the look of flames coming from the fire-breathing beast.

It was the Reynolds twins, one
wearing the dragon's head, the other
its body. The audience applauded
wildly. The judges scribbled furiously.

"Wow!" Harris whispered to his friends backstage. "That is a great costume. I guess we didn't see it before because they couldn't wear it at the same time in class!"

"You're next," Zeke whispered.

Harris clunked and clanked his way across the stage stiff-legged, with his antenna blinking brightly. Again, the audience applauded wildly and the judges made some notes.

Then it was Zeke's turn. He floated across the stage waving his tentacles in the air. His eyes bounced up and down, and he wiggled his antennae. Zeke got a nice round of applause, too.

When the last costumed student had crossed the stage, the judges gathered in a huddle. A few minutes later, they were ready to announce the winners.

Mr. Mulvaney stood up and spoke: "Third place goes to Zeke for his alien costume. Second place goes to Harris for his robot costume. And first place goes to the Reynolds twins for their amazing dragon costume!"

The audience gave another loud round of applause, and the winners were all given their medals.

10 TRICK OR TREAT!

"I DIDN'T WIN," ZEKE SAID, sounding surprised and a little disappointed.

"Sure you did," said Roxy. "Just because you didn't come in first doesn't mean you're not a winner."

"I'm happy," said Harris, pulling off his robot head. "I never won anything before. This is so cool!"

Roxy smiled.

"And Roxy," Harris continued. "I promise, next year, the three of us will make our costumes together."

"Yeah, and maybe next year, the three of us will win the top three spots!" said Roxy.

That night, the three friends, wearing the same costumes they wore to the contest, went out trick-or-treating together.

"Ooh," said one woman as she put candy into Zeke's bag. "That is a wonderful costume. Why, if I didn't know any better, I'd say you just landed here from another planet!"

"Thank you," said Zeke.

"I heard that Jeremy was grounded by his parents for that stunt with the flour," Harris said, as they moved onto the next house. "He's missing Halloween this year."

"It's funny, he was so concerned about Zeke's costume, but even Harris and the Reynolds twins beat Zeke!" Roxy said.

"Thanks for reminding me," Zeke said, and they all laughed.

At the next house, a man opened the door and said, "Nice costumes!" He turned to Zeke and asked, "What are you supposed to be?"

"I am supposed to be holding out my bag and getting candy from you," Zeke replied, straight-faced.

Harris and Roxy cracked up. Zeke didn't understand what was funny.

He still has a ways to go to understand humans! Harris thought.

"No, Zeke," said Roxy. "He means what is your costume."

"Oh," Zeke replied.

"He's an alien," Harris said.

Zeke smiled at Harris.

This is one time I can say that without giving away Zeke's secret, Harris thought. He could tell that Zeke was thinking the same thing.

Then the sorceress, the robot, and the alien, laughing and talking, moved on to the next house.

Read on for a sneak peek at the fifth book in the Alien Next Door series!

THE ALIEN NEXT DOOR

BASEBALL BLUES

5

BY A. I. NEWTON
ILLUSTRATED BY ANJAN SARKAR

HARRIS WALKER AND HIS BEST FRIEND Roxy Martinez burst out the front door of Harris's house. They clutched baseball gloves, a bat, and a ball in their hands.

The sun shone brightly. The last few patches of snow had melted. The first flowers had started to sprout, and a warm breeze mixed with the last of the chilly air.

"It's finally nice enough outside for the First Catch of the Year!" Harris said as he and Roxy ran to opposite sides of his front lawn.

The First Catch of the Year had been a tradition for Harris and Roxy since they were both old enough to throw a baseball.

Roxy took a few practice swings with her bat.

"I got this new bat for Christmas," she said. "I can't wait to use it!"

"And I got this new catcher's mitt," Harris said, pounding his fist over and over into the hard leather. "Time to break it in!"

Roxy put down her bat and slipped on her glove. She picked up the baseball and threw it right into Harris's mitt. It landed with a crisp, cracking sound.

"I can't wait for tryouts!" Harris cried. "I hope I get to play catcher this year."

Harris skipped a ground ball across the lawn. Roxy took two steps to her right, then reached over to field the ball backhanded.

"And I hope I get to play shortstop," Roxy said.

"Keep making plays like that and you'll be on the team for sure!" Harris said.

Harris and Roxy planned to try out for the Chargers, the local youth baseball team. The Chargers played against other teams from nearby towns.

Roxy tossed the ball high into the air. "Pop-up!" she yelled.

Harris looked up, raising his glove to shield the sun from his eyes. The ball started to come down.

"Hey, what are you guys doing?" asked a voice from behind Harris.

It was Zeke, Harris's new friend and next-door neighbor, who just happened to be an alien from the planet Tragas. Harris knew his secret. Roxy did not.

"Practicing baseball," Harris replied without taking his eyes off the ball. The pop-up landed in his glove with a soft thud.

"Base . . . ball?" Zeke asked.

"You don't have baseball in Tragas?!" Roxy asked.

Harris and Roxy gave Zeke a quick explanation of the sport. They talked about pitching, fielding, hitting, and running the bases.

Zeke smiled. "This sounds a lot like a game I used to play in Tragas," he said. "It's called Bonkas. Only in Bonkas, the bats are thinner and ten balls are put into play at the same time!"

"Ten balls!" Roxy exclaimed. "Boy, I have got visit Tragas some time."

"Well, it is pretty far away," Zeke said, glancing slyly at Harris.

If Roxy only knew how far! Harris thought.

"Hey, do you want to play catch, too?" Harris asked Zeke.

"I do," he said. "I miss playing Bonkas. But I don't have a glove."

"No problem," said Harris. He ran into the house and brought out one of his old gloves. "You can use this."

"Great!" said Zeke, slipping the glove onto his hand.

"Play ball!" shouted Harris.

A. I. NEWTON always wanted to travel into space, visit another planet, and meet an alien. When that didn't work out, he decided to do the next best thing—write stories about aliens! The Alien Next Door series gives him a chance to imagine what it's like to hang out with an alien. And you can do the same—unless you're lucky enough to live next door to a real-life alien!

ANJAN SARKAR graduated from Manchester Metropolitan University with a degree in illustration. He worked as an illustrator and graphic designer before becoming a freelancer, where he now gets to work on all sorts of different illustration projects! He lives in Sheffield, England.

anjansarkar.co.uk

LOOK FOR MORE BOOKS IN THE *ALIEN NEXT DOOR* SERIES!